Sian has been qualified in the field of specialised and therapeutic play for over 25 years, most of which has been within paediatrics and healthcare with children and young people. This is where she is most at home and is passionate about the role of normalising play and creativity enabling children and young people the space to share their story, or their worries.

Sharing and writing stories together is a joy, and Sian holds such impactful and important memories of these during her time supporting children, and young people during hospital stays.

Reducing trauma, through play and stories is powerful, and worries can be overwhelming.

The way they sit with children and young people, and the space they hold is one of the reasons she has decided to write this book, in the hope that the story can help children find the words.

Sian's other passions include working with young people, offering them a platform of support and care in supporting good mental health, as well as sharing her skills and knowledge with students and healthcare professionals.

Her current role is as Deputy Head of Play at Great Ormond Street Hospital for Children.

i

MUMBLES
AND THE
TALL TREE WOOD

SIAN SPENCER-LITTLE

AUSTIN MACAULEY PUBLISHERS™

LONDON · CAMBRIDGE · NEW YORK · SHARJAH

A CIP catalogue record for this title is available from the British Library.

ISBN 9781528941167 (Paperback)
ISBN 9781528970624 (ePub e-book)

www.austinmacauley.com

First Published 2023
Austin Macauley Publishers Ltd®
1 Canada Square
Canary Wharf
London
E14 5AA

iv

Listening to children and young people tell and share their stories, and offering safe spaces to play, and to be creative is one of the most powerful, and humbling things I have the privilege to do. Voices heard, honoured, and valued, enables a safe passage and an understanding of what matters to them and their lives.

This book is dedicated to many of my peers, to the children, young people and families who have trusted me.

To all who have listened, still listen, still empower, and to the courageous ones who have shared. To my loved ones, family, and friends.

Play Always Matters.

To the many teams of play, healthcare and education colleagues I have worked alongside, who strive to make a difference, I acknowledge the support and encouragement you have given me.

To the biggest influences in my professional life, the children, young people and families, for your courage, honesty and willingness to play.

Thank you.

This is Tall Tree Wood, and home to Mumbles the hedgehog and Doris the mouse.

Our story begins on a very cold night, not so long ago, when the grass crunched like crisps underneath your feet.

This is where Mumbles and Doris begin their adventures.

Let's see what happens?

Mumbles was sad; he had lived in Tall Tree Wood for such a long time but not always on his own.

He had some friends who had helped him, but they went away to visit Daisy Wood.

They said they would return but they never did, and Mumbles felt very lonely without them; he really wanted to find someone to talk to again.

He was looking for a friend who could help him as he was worried about a lot of things.

That's how he got his name.

Mumbles had heard that the other animals in Tall Tree Wood tell each other about him and the things he worries about.

When he didn't like something or when he felt worried, they could hear him mumbling to himself.

Things were so muddled for Mumbles.

Maybe, thought Mumbles , if I had a friend, I wouldn't get so lonely; and if they wanted to, they could help me with the things that make me so worried.

Today, as Mumbles crawled slowly through Tall Tree Wood, he could see that the sun was shining, and he made a whispering wish, "I wish the sun would shine all day and all night."

Then it wouldn't get dark.

Mumbles did not like the dark at all.

When he was worried it made his tummy feel like there was a thunderstorm inside it, and that made Mumbles very sad and very worried.

Mumbles would make himself as small as he could.

In the dark, Mumbles couldn't see where he was going or where anything was, and if he went to search for food, he would get lost, and would then have to sleep somewhere very strange.

Mumbles did not know what to do?

He remembered a long time ago that some big people came to Tall Tree Wood; it had started to get dark, and he worried that they wouldn't get home too, but one of them had a very bright light in his pocket.

What was this?

Things were so muddled for Mumbles.

Mumbles thought, *If only I could have one of those, I wouldn't be so worried about the dark, but how would I carry one, I only have little paws.*

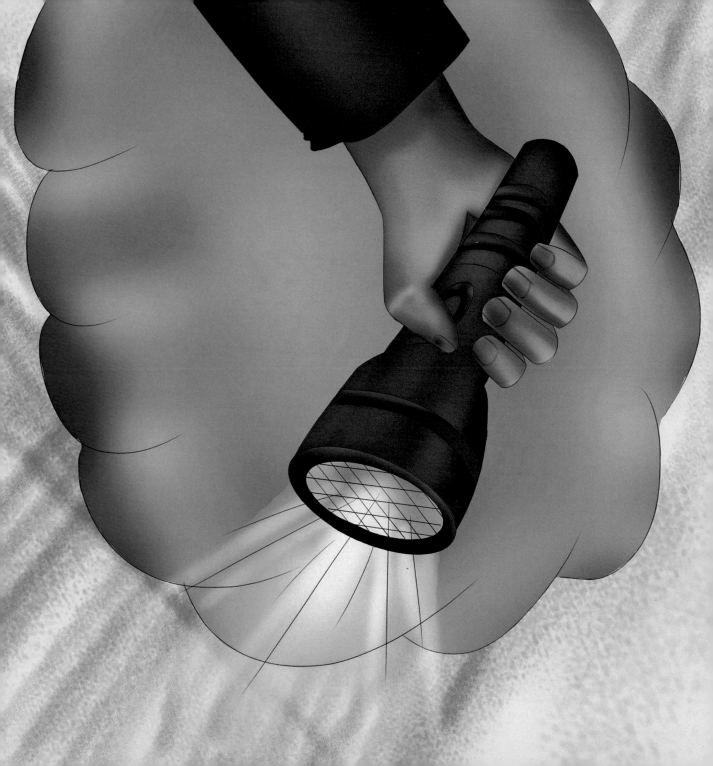

Just then Mumbles stopped.

He could see something in the leaves.

It was moving very quickly, what was it?

"Oh no, I don't like this; my tummy really hurts," mumbled Mumbles.

He couldn't move, he was so worried that he stuck to the forest floor like a statue, and he started to breathe really quickly, so quickly that he felt a bit dizzy.

Just then he saw a little face and some brown fur; it was hurrying towards him so quickly that he thought it might knock him over; he wanted to hide, but it was too fast and as it hurried past, he heard it say something,

"Morning, lots to do, can't stop."

It was so quick, Mumbles didn't have time to hide,

but he did feel sad as he wanted it to come back.

It was getting dark again, and so the worried tummy returned.

Things were so muddled for Mumbles.

As he settled down for the night, he thought he had heard a noise from outside the tree trunk he had found to sleep in.

A rustling noise, and then a ... *SQUEAK*.

Mumbles curled up like a ball and started to shake.

Out of the corner of his eye, he spotted some brown fur again.

"Hello Mr Hedgehog, my name is Doris."
Mumbles didn't say a word.
Doris moved closer.
"I said hello, what's the matter, why are you hiding?"

Mumbles felt all muddled inside, but with a wobbly voice and a deep breath he said, "My name is M—M—Mumbles. I can't come out, it's too dark out there."

Doris looked around Tall Tree Wood and said, "I used to get worried about the dark too, but one day I met some tiny creatures who are very beautiful and now they are my friends. I could take you to see them if you like; they really helped me and were very kind."

"NO, I can't!" shouted Mumbles which made Doris jump.

"You made me jump, you shouldn't be so cross," said Doris.

And with that, she hurried off into the woods.

Mumbles was all alone again and felt very sad.

He watched as the sun came up each day and then found a tree trunk to hide in as it went down each night.

Doris made a new house; it was very close to where Mumbles lived, but she hadn't seen him since he made her jump.

Doris thought about it some more. She wanted to visit Mumbles; it made her feel sad he was on his own and worried about the dark. This time, she would take some of her friends with her, so Mumbles could see how beautiful and kind they were.

Off she went; she really hoped that he didn't shout at her this time.

It had started to get dark but she could see where Mumbles lived, as the whole of the tree was shining. It sparkled like the stars; Doris was so glad she had asked her friends to visit.

She took a deep breath and knocked on Mumbles' tree trunk.

No answer.

Doris tried again, this time she heard a noise.

"Hello again, it's me Doris; I have brought some of my friends with me, the ones that helped me not be so worried about the dark."

Mumbles said nothing.

Slowly, the leaves began to move a little as a foot appeared.

Mumbles couldn't quite believe what was happening; he thought he was seeing things and rubbed his eyes with his paws.

All he knew was that it was dark and his tummy felt full with worry.

But all he could see were bright yellow lights.

They were beautiful.

As he moved from out of the tree, he still couldn't believe his eyes.

Where had the dark disappeared to?

"You see," said Doris, "I told you it would be OK and that I would help keep you safe. These are my friends, the fireflies; they help me to see in the dark so I don't get lost, and they are really friendly."

Tall Tree Wood looked beautiful.

Mumbles smiled at Doris and made himself jump as he had not smiled for a very long time.

He looked up; he didn't know that the trees were so tall.

The fireflies were so tiny but there was so many of them. For the first time ever, he wondered what it would be like to have so many friends and what adventures they would go on.

Mumbles suddenly did not feel so alone anymore.

He didn't feel so worried about the dark.

Mumbles was not so muddled now.

THE END

30